I Can't Do That, YET

Growth Mindset

Maima

Enna

Esther

Copyright © 2017 by Esther P Cordova
Illustrations by Maima W Adiputri

All rights reserved. www.powerofyet.com

Printed in the United States of America
First Printing, 2017
ISBN-13: 978-1545237274
ISBN-10: 1545237271

"It's bedtime, Enna!"

Enna loves all kinds of times: free time, play time, cookie time, and even brushing teeth time.

Bedtime is the time that Enna doesn't like. But, everybody knows that before bedtime, comes story time. And Enna loves story time.

Enna's dad asked her to read the first page. Like every evening, Enna responded, "I can't do that." Halfway through the story, Baxter crawled into the bed. Her dad pretended that he didn't notice.

Enna couldn't remember the end of the story. She must have fallen asleep but suddenly, she wasn't in her bed anymore.

She looked around and saw a woman. The woman was tall with long brown hair and glasses. Enna had the feeling she knew her. Somehow they must have met before.

"Finally, you are here. I was waiting for you all day long!" said the woman.

"Let me show you what we have done."
The woman smiled and took Enna by the hand.

"Look, Enna, this is our office. We usually arrive here at around nine in the morning. The team we work with is awesome. We hired a bunch of very creative and smart people.

Everybody works together, and we lead the technical department." Enna could tell that the woman was excited, but she had no idea what she was talking about. She didn't want to interrupt her, but she didn't understand why the woman kept saying we. Enna had never been here before. And why did the woman look so familiar?

"Yesterday was a crazy day. The servers went down, and everybody was worried. At first we couldn't find the problem in the code. Our web page wasn't showing anything. But, fortunately we were able to fix it in just twenty minutes!"

Enna was confused. She didn't know what servers were or why they were important, but she was glad that the woman was able to fix the problem.

Then the woman took Enna to a desk. There she turned on her computer and started writing something on a green background.

"Enna, I'm going to take a break. Can you finish the rest of the work?"

"Really?"

The woman started laughing, and Enna thought that was mean. But her laugh was so contagious that she eventually had to laugh too.

Suddenly, the woman got up and went to the fridge. She put celery sticks and a jar of peanut butter on the counter. Slowly the woman started to put a celery stick directly into the jar.

Enna's mom always told Enna to use a fork instead of putting the celery directly into the jar, but the woman didn't seem to care.

Enna still couldn't remember the woman's name. So she asked, "You are telling me all these things, but I don't even know your name."

The woman looked Enna in the eyes and said, "I'm you and you are me."

That was not possible. How can one person also be another person?

The woman stood up from her chair and whispered, "My name is Enna and I'm a possible version of you in the future. The only thing different about you and me is TIME."

Enna was confused. "That can't be true. I don't even know what you are talking about. Server, code ... I can't do any of that."

"You can't do that? Enna, you can't do that YET because you haven't had the time that I've had. When we were sixteen, we started to learn computer programming. We made this little game and every-thing went from there. You really wanted this, and so you created me, just like you created this game."

"But, I don't remember any of that."

"How could you? This is the future. If you want this, it could be YOUR future."

Enna couldn't believe what she had just heard. How could all of this be possible? She wasn't like this woman, at all. But maybe she really could be like her. This future seemed exciting.

Enna had so many thoughts at once that she wasn't able to say anything. The woman said that Enna could be her if she wanted. But what if she didn't want to be her?

Enna didn't want to hurt her older self's feelings; so, she didn't say anything.

Enna's older self looked at her and said gently, "You don't need to say anything. I know exactly how you feel. I want you to meet a few people before you have to go. All of them care about you very much."

With these words, she opened a door wide, and Enna could see what was inside. The room was full of Ennas. There were so many Ennas that she didn't know which one to focus on first.

ach one seemed different but at the same time similar. Nobody seemed to notice little Enna. She wished she vere able to stay forever and to meet every single one of them. Just when she finally had the courage to step into the room full of Ennas, the door closed.

Suddenly, Enna's feet started to feel wet. She heard a voice far away. The voice told her that she had to go now. She then heard her older self telling her one last thing: "We are always inside you, even when you don't see, feel, or know it."

Enna felt Baxter licking her feet and quickly realized that she was back in her bed.

She got up right away and told her dad, "I want to try to read the first page tonight. With a little time I'll get it right. I just can't do it, yet."

I can't do that, YET

Made in the USA
Monee, IL
09 September 2019